GW01325992

# I Must Confess...
## And Other Short Stories

Laura Goodsell

authorHOUSE®

*AuthorHouse™ UK Ltd.*
*500 Avebury Boulevard*
*Central Milton Keynes, MK9 2BE*
*www.authorhouse.co.uk*
*Phone: 08001974150*

*© 2009 Laura Goodsell. All rights reserved.*

*No part of this book may be reproduced, stored in a retrieval system, or transmitted by any means without the written permission of the author.*

*First published by AuthorHouse 7/16/2009*

*ISBN: 978-1-4389-9649-3 (sc)*

*This book is printed on acid-free paper.*

To Sue, Gerry and Jamie, who, throughout writing this book, have supported me whole heartedly.
Thank you

# *Biography*

I had always wanted to write, it wasn't until a couple of years ago I decided to embrace the art, and took a short story creative writing course; I have been hooked ever since.

This is my first book, and definitely won't be my last.

I hope you enjoy it.

You can find other information, or leave me feedback at my website www.lauragoodsell.co.uk

A big thank you to all of you for buying this book.

All photos taken by: **Laura Goodsell**
Front cover artist: **Audrey Clarke**

# Contents

## I Must Confess...

'Can I buy one ticket to Norwich Please?'

Charlotte liked to think she was feeling quite positive, considering the circumstance, but really, deep down there was a mass of emotions she wasn't quite sure what to do with, and just wanted to get today over.

She knew she'd been taking a huge risk doing what she did, but Charlotte just couldn't let someone get away with Murder.

When today was over, and she could get back to her little cottage in the sticks, she knew she would struggle to put it all behind her, but she would be on safe grounds. She could lock herself away as she always did in a crisis, she had learnt to ignore problems and they would eventually go away.

But this had been different. It was her sister.

Taking her ticket, she picked up her over night bag, and swung her handbag back over her shoulder. Walking towards the train platform, she couldn't quite understand why she had that butterfly feeling in her stomach she used to get as a child, right before she climbed on to the big merry go round at the fun fair. Oh! How they had loved that fun fair; life had seemed so happy and uncomplicated.

'I'm fine, I'm going to be just fine,' she whispered under her breath trying to think more positively.

'All Aboard, All Aboard!' shrilled the platform Master. Charlotte hurriedly picked up speed, half running, half hobbling, struggling with her bags, and making it to the train's steps just in time. Feeling out of breath Charlotte pretty much fell into the first carriage she came to.

By the time she got her bearings and her breath back; she could feel her heart beating in her mouth. She realised that there were only two other people in the carriage with her; an elderly grey haired lady and a young business man in a smart grey suit, thoroughly engrossed in his newspaper.

After stowing her overnight bag in the racks above her, she flopped herself onto the seat next to the window. Charlotte took a few deep breaths and leaned back.

'Clunk, Clunk, Clunk,' the train started to move out slowly. With a loud guttural whistle and a huge blast of white steam floating by the carriage windows, they were away.

After several long silent minutes, the elderly lady sitting opposite Charlotte started to rummage around in her big patchwork bag that was sat on her lap, and produced a bag of mint humbugs. With a gentle smile and extended hand she asked 'Would you like one dear?'

'Thank you so much, I would love one, I'm Charlotte by the way.' Taking a sweet herself and tucking the bag away, the elderly lady replied 'Nice to meet you, I'm Grace.' She produced her latest knitting project, a tangle of pink and purple fluffy wool, and enthusiastically started telling Charlotte about it, but Charlotte only listened half heartedly, she just couldn't seem to get her sister out of her mind.

After a while they fell into an easy conversation, covering all manner of topics including the weather and favourite authors they had in common. They quickly passed the time away.

'Are you visiting family Charlotte?' eventually asked Grace.

'Uh no, I'm not visiting family.' Charlotte started to fidget, feeling herself getting a little hot and convinced she was probably bright red with it too. She sat on her hands to try to stop herself fidgeting.

'Are you just on a shopping trip?' Grace probed further. Still reeling from her sister's death, Charlotte wasn't too comfortable talking about it. Yet she knew she had to talk to someone, it was driving her round the bend keeping it to her self.

If only she had had a family of her own, but that chance had long gone, along with her cheating husband, thank God!

On one hand she just wanted to bury all her thoughts deep within herself and never release them, on the other hand she liked this lady.

Grace. She had something about her, summing her up, Charlotte thought; Curly white hair, rimless glasses propped on the end of her nose, bright eyes, a bit chunky round the middle, comforting smile, her whole comfortable grandma persona.

Charlotte thought, I do feel at ease being here chatting to her. She seems willing to listen, and we do have a long old train journey ahead of us, anyway it might help me to talk to someone with an outsiders view.

Grace sat quietly watching Charlotte, with her head tipped to one side.

'I am just visiting Norwich, but not for a happy occasion. Like visiting family,' Charlotte eventually confided, 'I'm going to my sister Clio's funeral, later on today.'

'Oh my, I'm so sorry dear.' Grace looked at Charlotte with those bright eyes, a touch of sympathy was now visible, and she reached forward and patted her on the hand in a strangely comforting way.

'I didn't mean to pry, are you ok, do you need a tissue?'

'Its ok, I'm fine, thank you,' Charlotte was trying hard to blink back the tears that were now beginning to sting her eyes.

'Please don't feel bad you weren't to know. Unfortunately we weren't as close as we should have been,' said Charlotte feeling slightly uncomfortable, yet relieved with her small, but she felt none the less dramatic revelation.

'Do you mind me asking how she died?' enquired Grace.

'Well,' this was the bit Charlotte was most dreading.

'She was murdered, it's quite a long story, but the man who did it, is now going to spend life behind bars, hopefully,' said Charlotte as Grace's eyes widened in amazement. An awkward look became slightly apparent on her face.

'Oh my, she couldn't have been very old.'

'No she wasn't, she was my little sister, only turned twenty three a few weeks ago.'

Charlotte looked down at the grubby carriage carpet, suddenly feeling unsure of herself, and the realisation of the last few weeks' began to really sink in.

'Its been the most terrifying and unreal time of my life. It still doesn't feel as though it actually really happened to me. It kind of feels like it's somebody else's life, and I've been watching it all play out from up above. I guess I could admit, in a strange way it has been sort of exciting, I have felt emotions I never knew existed.

'Nothing ever happens in my life, I lead a very dull existence,' she explained quietly, not wanting this lady to think she found her sisters death exciting in any way. Grace sat quietly, nodding, listening intently, unsure of what to say, or even if she should say anything at all.

'Well, as I said before,' Charlotte carried on, 'Clio and I had never really been close. She ran away a long, long time ago, when we were quite young, she was a bit of a troublesome child, my mother use to say. She was lured away by the bright lights of the city. I had seen her a couple times since she left, but Clio never got on with my husband, and that unfortunately, caused a lot of rows between us. Now, that was about a year ago, and we haven't spoken since. Now we never will. But I've slowly come to terms with it, and hopefully see the funeral as closure, where I can say my final goodbye.'

Grace looked at Charlotte sympathetically, 'That's so sad, family are so very important. You said your sister was murdered? How did it happen if you don't mind me asking, it's just things like that don't happen around here?'

'Uh, well, if I start at the beginning, it will all make more sense; you'll probably read about it in the papers soon anyway. The police have kept it out of the public eye up until now because of this guy's Fathers political standing.'

'Really!' Grace perked up at this new revelation, 'I'm getting more intrigued by the minute.'

'Oh, ok, uh,' Charlotte Stammered, feeling a bit surprised by Graces interest, nobody had ever quite taken so much interest in her before.

'I had the police knock on my door on a Tuesday morning, and they told me Clio had died. Apparently Clio's landlady, Marcy, had told them she had a sister, and gave them my address. She also later told me Clio used to talk about me all the time. Why she never got in touch with me I'll now never know. I guess she was scared. We hadn't left things on a good note. Although I would have done anything to help her,' Charlotte paused, reflecting.

'I really liked that she still thought of me, though,' she said quietly.

'Anyway I had to go and identify her, and collect her belongings, I didn't want some stranger going through her things, plus I felt I owed her this, as I hadn't been there for her when she needed me most. I also met her landlady, Marcy at that point. She was really nice, she said she thought highly of Clio, and let me stay in Clio's flat until I was sorted. Well I say flat, it was a basement room with a sink, shower, cooker and bed. It was really horrible, a bit to dark and damp, with mouldy patches above the doors. You can guess I wasn't planning on staying there too long.'

At this point the train started to slow down into the next station and the well dressed business man sitting opposite, gathered up his belongings, gave Charlotte a quick nervous glance and left the carriage.

Charlotte and Grace were now alone.

'Would you like another humbug?' offered Grace, rummaging around in her patchwork bag, after the train slowly started to move out again.

'Oh thank you.' Charlotte picked one from the bag.

'Well,' Charlotte continued, 'I started to pack up Clio's things and came across quite a few letters from some guy called Rupert Hemmingway. At this point I had no idea who he was, but I asked Marcy, and she did know!'

'Oh yes, he's quite well known around these parts,' cut in Grace, a little too stiffly thought Charlotte.

'Yes well, that concerned me a bit; you see these letters were more like lovers letters,' she said slowly, 'I felt quite bad reading them, I could tell Clio had replied to these, just by the way they were written.' Charlotte saw Graces face, falsely taking her expression for surprise.

'I was surprised myself. I thought I've got to talk to this man, if he was my sister's lover, then did he even know she had died? And if he did how come he hadn't come forward? So I tried to see him on several occasions, and got the same response from his secretary every time; that he was too busy to see me. I told his secretary I was Clio's sister, and that I needed to speak with him urgently. She said she had never heard of my sister. It started to sound a bit strange to me.'

'Did you get to see him?' Grace cut in.

'Yes. I did, and it wasn't a pleasant experience I can tell you, he was not a nice man,'

Grace raised her eyebrows, 'Oh Really?'

'No. He came bustling in when I was at the flat packing up the last few bits of Clio's things, and do you know what he said to me?' She was really getting into the swing of things now.

'He warned me to stay away and to stop harassing his secretary! He did say he was sorry Clio had died, "but these things happen to people in her line of work,"' she mimicked in a posh accent, 'Which I though was a bit strange. But it soon became clear. I don't know why I didn't see it earlier.' Charlotte sat with her head in her hands. 'The so called flat she lived in, the few tatty and rather revealing clothes she owned, and the money I found in the back of her wardrobe.' Charlotte Paused looked up and outside into the rain soaked fields.

'Well, what did you find out?'

'She was a lady of the night,' whispered Charlotte. 'I can't think of a nicer way to put it, this man never admitted it, but I knew he was one of her customers, He seemed to be hiding something, or so I though. My head was all over the place.' Charlotte paused.

'I decided I wasn't going to leave town until I knew how my sister had died. This guy had just confirmed that something wasn't quite right. He was very anxious for me to leave. I decided to go back to see him, but this time I confided in a local policeman whom Macy had put me in contact with. He was a lovely guy and seemed really sympathetic, it seems that the police department just put it down to another "murdered call girl," so they weren't too concerned with the case's priority, but he came with me as this guy Rupert, was a bit hot tempered and I didn't trust him.

'Anyway PC Watson and I went to Rupert's home, I was armed with the letters he had sent Clio hoping to get him to admit to something, but I never expected what I actually got.

'I started to push him, asking questions. I couldn't help It, I had been thinking about it for a while, and kind of built up a picture as to how the confrontation was going to play out; I was calm for a starters and he would confess. But as in real life, my mind went blank and I got really angry thinking, this guy had something to do with Clio's death, and I wanted to know what it was.' Charlotte seemed to really loose herself in telling her tale now.

'After a while of me shouting questions at him, I think he just cracked under the pressure. I guess it's a pretty big thing to carry around with you, I think I was just the final straw. Well he confessed, he completely confessed to killing Clio! It just came out. How it was an accident, he didn't mean to do it; she had just driven him round the bend. All her talk of going public, buying a place together, He had just lashed out.

'I think he finally realised what he'd done, he just broke down. PC Watson came in with his handcuffs and took him away. He didn't try to fight it at all, he just followed with his head bowed and his shoulders slumped forward.

'Clio had fallen in love with this guy, and he killed her for it, all he saw her as was a quick fling. Although I guess looking at who his father is, he couldn't be seen to be seeing someone in Clio's line of work; it would have ruined his father. But still he didn't have to kill her...

'So here I am. Here for Clio's funeral, with her killer hopefully behind bars for a very long time, I feel I can really say goodbye properly now.'

Looking across at Grace, out the corner of her eye, she wondered what she was thinking, as she was now sitting very quiet and still, as though she wanted to say something but couldn't find the right words. She had been listening intently, and seemed interested, or at least that's what Charlotte had thought.

'Are you ok?' she ventured.

'Yes dear, I'm fine,' Grace seemed to be forcing a wide smile at Charlotte. She looked down at her watch and realised they would be pulling into the station at any moment, 'I better get my things together were nearly there,' Grace mumbled.

The train started to slow down and sounded a very loud whistle to signal its arrival.

'I do apologise. This whole journey I've been talking about myself, and my problems. Would you like to get a coffee? I have a couple hours before I need to meet Marcy,' Charlotte asked.

Grace looked touched, 'that sounds like a lovely idea, but I do apologise, I really need to be somewhere this afternoon, maybe another time? Are you staying in Norwich long or do you need to get home?'

'No, no I'm going to be staying for a few days,' Charlotte replied.

'Well, let me give you my details, and maybe we could go for that coffee.'

'Yes ok, here, I have a pad and a pen somewhere.'

Charlotte rummaged in her own bag and produced a small pocket book and pencil.

As Grace scribbled down her details, Charlotte accidentally elbowed her bag off the seat and onto the floor. 'Damn!'

In her rush to collect her things together, the contents spilled everywhere. Annoyed, she grabbed everything up, made sure she had her letter; it had the address on it for the funeral home she had to visit. Just as she was on her hands and knees, in the middle of the carriage, looking for her change purse that had fallen under the seat, the train came to a jolting stop.

'Are you ok down there dear the train has stopped, and I'm afraid I have to leave now.' Grace stared down at Charlotte.

'Oh right of course,' feeling a bit flustered she stood up, clutching her bag and brushed herself down.

Grace looked deep into her eyes, held her arms, and gave her a really big hug.

'Please don't worry about anything, everything will be alright. I can assure you he has gotten what he deserves, but family is very, very important, and I have to be there for him now, at this very difficult time, but, believe me, I do not condone what happened to your poor, poor sister at all.'

Charlotte pulled back from Grace with a look of complete confusion, 'I'm sorry, I don't understand. What do you mean? Who do you need to be there for? And what was that about family?' She said rather puzzled.

'All will become clear my dear, if you write me I promise I will write back.' Grace folded the small pocket book into Charlotte's hand, kissed her on the cheek, slid back the compartment door, and left Charlotte, looking and feeling very confused, standing in the compartment on her own, staring after Grace.

Looking down at her note book she stared in disbelief at what Grace had written.

It said, 'I apologise. I don't have the courage to tell you myself. But I'm Rupert Hemmingway's Grandmother. I should have told you earlier but I just couldn't. I have grown very fond of you on this short journey. Please don't blame yourself for what happened, I hate to say it, but he deserved the punishment he got for what he did to your sister, and the grief he has caused, please write me and I will answer any questions you may have.' with that Grace had left her address at the bottom.

'Oh dear god! I just told his grandmother everything.' Charlotte started to feel very angry at her self, 'What was I thinking telling a total stranger, I should have known better,' she said out loud. Standing stock still in the middle of the empty carriage Charlotte thought long and hard about Grace and her own revelation.

She did say she didn't blame me. She should hate me; I put her grandson behind bars! But she doesn't. Charlotte went out into the hall way and started to make her way from the train. She found all this very hard to take in. Wrestling very much with her emotions, thinking; Grace has shown me great courage, and she wants me to stay in contact, plus she's standing by her grandson even though she doesn't agree with what he has done, wow! This is all too much to take in right now.

Charlotte stepped off the train.

I'll stay in contact with Grace. If she can forgive me, then maybe one day I can forgive Rupert and get rid of some of this anger I feel towards him. She slowly made her way through the crowds of people, not really seeing anyone.

'I can do this,' she said out loud. Not looking forward to her sister's funeral at all, but feeling slightly more at ease with her self.

She felt a stronger person emotionally. With a slight smile on her lips, she walked out of the station.

## *Crossing Over*

Megan had no idea what had just happened, one moment she was admiring a fantastic pair of black leather boots in a shop window, the next she was on the floor, with a nasty bump on her head.

Slowly pushing her self up into a sitting position she reached a hand to the back of her head, it ached and her vision was a bit blurry. Wobbling as she stood up, Megan couldn't see her bag anywhere. Ducking down she checked under the parked cars and looked in doorways, she even peered down the drains in desperation, but it was nowhere to be seen. Clutching her dizzy forehead, she figured that it must have been stolen; all of a sudden the panic set it.

A thousand thoughts ran through her mind, where is it? Has someone stolen it? Was I robbed? Knocked down? Or did I faint and then get robbed? What's going on?

Steadying herself against a shop window, Megan took a deep breath, and brushed the bits of dirt and grit from her trousers. Deciding to report her bag stolen, she headed in the direction of the local police station. I'll report my cards stolen when I get home, she thought.

Walking down the path Megan noticed the November air had warmed up slightly, she didn't feel cold anymore; come to think of it she didn't feel warm either.

An ambulance, sirens blaring, literally flying down the street snapped her out of her day dream.

The police station wasn't too much of a walk, it was soon in sight.

A couple of boys in dark hooded tops, with their jeans hanging round their bums, were skulking around the court house doors, which had been built onto the side of the police station, trying as they might to look hard and cool. 'Lazy layabouts' Megan mumbled.

They did scare Megan slightly, she didn't like the way they kept there faces covered by their hood's, and why oh why, did they have to have their jeans hanging so low! Megan as you can guess was a little old before her time. She was only twenty six.

She then remembered an article she had read in a newspaper about the so called "local celebrity yob" being in town this week, no wonder everyone was in such a rush, this was a pretty big thing for such a small town, She thought.

Pulling open the huge double doors Megan stepped inside to a thick fug of stale smoke and busy conversation, it was packed, she couldn't see where the front desk was for all the people, flashing cameras, shouts and ringing phones. A lot of policemen were rushing everywhere, policemen rushing, that was unusual in itself.

After stepping into the station, of which she couldn't get much further than the threshold, looking around her she noted that no one was taking the slightest bit of notice of her. No matter how hard she tried, and how loud she raised her voice, or who she spoke to, it didn't make any difference. Giving up she decided to try again later, thinking, maybe she would call them from home, so she walked back into town.

Spotting one of her old school friends, who she hadn't seen for years, Megan waved hoping to at least get a wave back; nothing, slightly baffled she thought, maybe she didn't recognise me; it could be my new hair cut. Never mind, today's been a bit of a disaster anyway, I can't even ring anyone to come and pick me up, as my phone was in my damn bag!

Deciding to have one last look for her bag, she headed back towards the shop with the fantastic boots, feeling a bit sorry for her self, as she now can't afford to buy them; not having any cash or cards.

She was a little lost in her thoughts, staring at the ground as she walked, so she nearly didn't notice all the commotion up ahead of her. A bit similar to the mass of people at the police station apart from these people also included paramedics, and an ambulance. Plus lots of onlookers, shocked and horrified, some even crying. Getting closer to have a look, she saw two paramedics wheeling what looked like a covered body into the back of an ambulance. It was weird, as this was the exact same place that, Megan, only 30 minutes ago was knocked down.

Although she still wasn't sure what had happened, only that her head hurt, and her bag was missing.

'They should maybe do something about this spot. Two people in the same day, it's a danger zone,' Megan said to the old lady next to her, who was craning her neck around the crowd. Sadly thinking, only this poor person wasn't quite as lucky as me.

She started scanning the crowd; people were now beginning to disperse, as all the action was now in the ambulance. Leaving only a few behind, Megan noticed someone waiting with the paramedics to get into the ambulance, 'That's my Sister, Oh My God!' she felt her heart jump up into her throat, 'Maybe I know them! Rachel, Rachel!' she called, her head was spinning again, but her sister just turned her back and got into the waiting ambulance.

Running towards Rachel, she jumped up into the ambulance just in time, as the last paramedic swung the door shut, she was pretty sure that her foot had only just left the floor when the door swung closed, but it didn't hit her.

Sitting down next to her sister, still looking puzzled at the door, she thought No, I must have been mistaken, shaking her head as if to try and clear it of any more strange thoughts, she turned to her crying sister and asked 'Who is it Rachel? What's going on, why did you ignore me out their?' but received no response.

'This is ridiculous! I'm not squeamish,' looking at the body, and then back to her sister who was now rummaging round in her bag, Megan decided to have a peek, her curiosity had gotten the better of her, she had to know who it was. Bending forward she tried to lift the sheet up; but she received the strangest cold sensation that she had ever had, her hand just fell straight through It. it felt like she had just plunged her hand in a bucket of ice cold water.

Yelling. Panicked, she jumped to her feet; the ambulance rounded a corner, she fell backwards against the side, but hurt herself? In fact she didn't feel a thing.

Steadying herself with her arms outstretched, and a look of absolute horror fixed to her face, she re-played, in her mind, her hand going through the sheet, and just screamed. Heart pounding, she couldn't breathe, standing up as much as she could, with the ambulance moving, she tried again to lift the cover.

She desperately tried to convince herself her hand had just missed it. But there it was, straight through again, 'What the hell!' then she heard voices, a familiar voice, muffled and quiet at first, but then it became louder, it was coming from her sister. Megan had actually forgotten she was sitting their, what was she saying? She was talking about her, what has happened!

'Mum I'm so, so, sorry Mum, there's been an accident, it's Megan, and I'm with her now on the way to the uh, hospital, please come quickly, she's.....' Megan couldn't make out the rest, her sister just burst into sobs of tears, she was still talking, but it was unintelligible. She tried to listen, but her mind wouldn't let her, she had to see who was under the white sheet, it was a matter of life or death, literally!

For the rest of the Journey, Megan just sat with her head in her hands, trying to make some logical sense, of all the information swirling round inside her, it felt like some kind of emotional tornado, the more she thought, the more messed up it seemed.

Soon the ambulance lurched to a stop outside the emergency entrance. When the paramedic pulled back the double doors, Megan jumped out and followed all the commotion into the hospital, watching as her sister signed in. She was then taken into a side room by an official looking man. The A & E was pretty crowded but Megan didn't notice. Her mind felt numb, she walked slowly through the crowd and stared through the glass mesh at her sister talking to the doctor. It didn't look good.

Not long after, her Mum and Dad hurried in through the door and joined her sister, they looked so sad. Megan could see the official looking guy through the window was comforting her sister. I so want to be with them, and hug them, and comfort them, I really need my parents right now, I'm so scared and feel so lonely, Megan thought, and then she started to cry, or she felt the emotion of crying, but no tears streamed down her face.

Just then, her family got up, the doctor lead them out of the little room, and down a corridor. Megan followed really close by, desperate to reach out to her Mother, but afraid at what might happen if she did. They all turned left down another long corridor, and then down a flight of steps. Eventually they stopped and entered a room with a small sign attached to it "Mortuary."

Megan felt her heart jump up into her mouth when she saw it. Her eyes lingered on the sign, as everyone filed in. She went after them; the room was very clean and tidy, also extremely bright. Megan noticed her Mum and sister squinting a bit before their eyes adjusted to the glare: the light didn't affect Megan.

She couldn't help looking at the shiny metal table in the middle of the room, her eyes were drawn to the covered body on top, she could feel her heart beating, was surprised nobody else could her it; it was like a marching band drumming in her ears.

The doctor was talking to her Mum; Megan was unable to hear him over the beating. He walked forward, stretched out his hand, and lifted the cloth, slowly, and pulled it back up to the neck. It couldn't, it just couldn't! Megan Reeled, her head was spinning; her whole world went black and felt like it was imploding.

'No, No, No, Mum I'm fine! I'm here!'
she was shouting, now screaming, but
nobody listened, nobody could hear.
Her Mum was crying and her sister
was comforting her; she draped her
arm around her Mum's shoulders, and
led her out of the room, nodding to
the doctor as she went. Megan's Dad
followed silently, his head was bowed.

The door closed, and Megan was
alone, suddenly realising she hadn't
moved since setting eyes on herself
lying on the table. She gave a little
start and averted her gaze, did this
mean she was dead! It couldn't, she
wouldn't believe it! 'That's me!' She
said out loud, nearly hysterical. She
cautiously stepped closer, 'It really is
me, I don't want to be dead, but, but,
look at me!' at this point she broke
down, the realisation hitting her hard.
It was at this point Megan spotted her
bag sitting by her feet, she felt like
laughing, but dropped to her knees
and curled up into the foetal position
instead.

What about my family and all the
things I wanted to do? What about
my Mum and Dad! What's going to
happen now? Where do I go? I'll never
experience children or a husband, so
many things undone. Do I wander

around forever, nobody being able to see me? So many mixed thoughts ran through her mind.

Looking through the glass door to her parents Megan thought, they look so sad, and it's because of me, I've hurt them beyond words, I don't even understand how I died! Was it a car accident, it must have been. There's nothing I can do for them now, at least they have each other.

Megan was starting to feel calmer, a strange kind of calm that seemed to engulf her whole body, it's ok, it's really ok, I'm going to be ok, my family is going to be ok, at last she felt she was beginning to understand. Everything seemed to be making sense; she knew what she had to do now.

Turning to face the far wall, it was glowing bright, brighter than the rest of the room, the white light seemed to be shimmering, she knew she had to walk towards it, just knew it, Megan felt her self being pulled towards it, like her whole body was magnetised, the closer she got the more calm she felt, everything seemed content, comfortable, just so.

As she walked forward Megan thought of the life she was leaving behind; she would miss her parents terribly, although she knew they would be fine. She would miss them so much, but this was the way she needed to go. Someone or something, was telling her it was right.

The peace and comfort she felt as she continued walking towards the glow felt really wonderful. She continued walking until the room was empty and silent; the only sounds were the muffled distant commotions, of every day life outside. Everyone unaware of the journey Megan was about to undertake into the next life.

## *Second Chances*

It was a bitter cold night; the dark was piercing and the moon was covered by clouds, tiny spots of rain fell every now and then, threatening more. Exactly the kind of night Scott loved; he could sneak about the park and not get spotted, as nobody else would be out in this weather.

Ducking from tree to tree, so as not to be seen, although it didn't really matter, he finally found what he was looking for, the entrance to his den. It was hidden in a blackberry bramble bush and was a bit painful to get in but it was worth it. As he scrambled in, he heard a ripping noise, turning around he noticed he'd caught his backpack on the thorns, the zip had broken and he'd lost his torch light. Feeling around on the ground he couldn't find it, Damn! He though, Oh well I'll get it tomorrow, it's too dark and windy to look tonight.

Scott loved the privacy his den gave him; not having many friends, he found being alone in his den, in his own fantasy world; well, it helped keep the real world outside and away from him. It was his protection. His sanctuary.

There was a lot more shelter in the den; he could hear the wind howling outside. He slumped down into his comfy armchair, and picked up the battered old guitar he had found in a dumpster a few months back, he started to string a few cords together, into a song he had been working on, when a strange noise caught his attention over the wind. Scott leaned the guitar against a tree stump, and strained to hear.

He couldn't quite make it out; was it a cat? Something was definitely out there; Scott could hear his heart pounding. Suddenly a flash of bright light streaked through his den, a face appeared dark and distorted through the brambles as if from nowhere, 'Hey!!! Who are you?' The voice was angry.

Scott jumped up and ran. Knowing his den had been violated, he wanted to get the hell out of there as soon as possible, he squeezed back through the brambles, not caring how many thorns pricked him, or how much he was bleeding. He just kept on running, out of the park, across the main road, past the shops, until he reached his home; with a pain in his chest like nothing he had felt before, it took him a few moments, doubled over, to get his breath back.

Terrified of what he saw and heard, he just went straight up to bed, his heart felt like it was going to explode, it was beating so fast he could feel the blood rushing in his head, he needed to just hide from the world.

The next morning Scott ventured out of his room around nine thirty, knowing that his Dad would be out at work at the timber factory; he was always out working, it made Scott feel ever so more lonely.

Downstairs, Scott popped a couple slices of bread in the toaster, and sat at the dining table while he waited for it to pop. Sitting in the silent kitchen, vivid flashes crossed his mind of last night; he couldn't sleep because of it, so his eyes stung this morning. Scott knew he was being silly, but that den meant the world to him and now it was lost.

The toast popped and he slapped some butter on it, then headed out the back door eating. Even though he was scared the night before, the daylight made everything seem ok again. He wanted to get back to his den to see if anything was salvageable, and to find out if that guy had done anything.

Wrapped up in his scarf and gloves, as the wind and cold hadn't yet died down. Scott walked along the familiar route taken so many times before; he felt an uneasy sensation in the pit of his stomach.

Standing there staring at the bramble bush he thought, It looked like the old den but it didn't feel like it. The glint in the wet grass caught his eye; he bent down to pick it up. It looked like an old stop watch - possibly gold and expensive - he wondered what that man was up to down here last night, and why this watch was here. He didn't know and didn't really want to, as the mystery cut into his routine of hiding. Although it did intrigue him, he liked to think he had an adventurous side... hidden somewhere.

Scott put together the few belongings he had in his den, but had to leave behind the old sofa armchair that had a huge rip down the side; it was still quite comfortable and lovely to snuggle up in.

On his way home with his carrier bags of belongings, he remembered the watch was still in his pocket. He decided to pop into the local watch shop to see if it was worth anything, if he could maybe get ten pounds for it that would be worth it.

The dust hit his lungs as soon as the door creaked open, and he heard a light ping come from out the back of the shop. He looked around and felt a shiver run down his spine, this place was awful. Old dusty cabinets full of pocket watches and a few with crappy looking books. Just then an old man with thick white hair and tiny gold rimmed glasses came out of what looked like a stock cupboard.

'My name is Mr Dobson, How can I help young man?'

'Well I found something; can you tell me if it's worth anything?'

'Ok let's have a look.' Mr Dobson laid down the book he was carrying and stepped forward. Scott pulled out the pocket watch and laid it on the counter for Mr Dobson to see.

'Well, let's have a look here,' He picked up a tiny magnifying glass, and leaned over the glass top counter to get a closer look, 'Well,' Mr Dobson said again, 'this is certainly interesting. It is valuable.'

'How much is it worth? I know it must be worth something...I hope.'

'Yes. How did you come across it?' Mr Dobson looked suspiciously at Scott over the rim of his specs.

'Well, I found it, on the ground, up by the park.'

'I see, now. I know this watch, it's rare and I'm afraid stolen,' Mr Dobson eyed Scott again. 'I will need to call the police.' Scott edged back towards the door, feeling slightly queasy.

'Uh, if you found it and didn't steel it yourself, you wouldn't mind staying here and talking to them would you? You may be able to offer them some help.' Mr Dobson stepped towards Scott.

Panicking Scott realised he didn't really want to have an adventure after all and needed to hide. He turned and ran.

'Stop! Wait a moment stop don't go!' Shouted Mr Dobson, but Scott was out the door and down the street before the old man could move.

Unfortunately for Scott, Mr Dobson had recognised him, and knew his father. It was a small town where everyone knew everyone else's business. So he closed up his shop; just for a few moments, to have a word with Mavis Orton, who was the receptionist at the local high school. As the schools were on holiday, he guessed that she would be home, and would know exactly where Scott lived. But before he visited Scott he thought he should call the local police station, as he knew that watch had been stolen from him the previous night. He didn't care so much about the other stuff that was taken but that watch was of great sentimental value to him.

So he dialled an officer he knew he could trust at the local station 'Hello, is that Inspector Bradford? I have some information for you regarding the break-in at my shop yesterday. Yes that's it; I think I may have a lead for you. A young lad found my watch, it's in my shop. I was wondering if you could have a look at it and see if it still has any prints on. I haven't touched it, so hopefully there will be something for you to use. No the young lad who found it is very shy. I'm now on my way to see him... ok thank you. Could you come and collect the watch? It's on the counter in my shop; I'll leave the spare keys with the lady who runs the book shop next door.'

About half an hour later he was on his way down the high street, to the large housing estate at the north end of town. It took about twenty minutes as they all look the same, but he eventually found Scott's house, and went and knocked on the door. Scott's Dad Dave, answered; it was his afternoon off work. 'Yeah, who are you?'

'My name is Mr Dobson, Sorry to barge in like this, but I was wondering if your son was home? He came into my shop earlier; I run the watch shop on the high street? Is he home?'

'Yeah, what do you want with him?' Dave narrowed his eyes, and pulled the door to.

'I need to speak with him about an item he brought into my shop earlier today,'

'What item?'

'I think I should really speak with him direct, thank you.' Mr Dobson stood firm.

'Fine come on in then, want a cuppa?' said Dave, moving from the door.

'Yes, thank you that would be nice.'

Dave wandered through to the kitchen as Mr Dobson glanced around the small living room. He noticed that it was quite untidy; newspapers and magazines were scattered around, along with half drunk cups of tea, he wasn't overly impressed.

Scott appeared in the doorway, slouched against the frame, arms crossed. Mr Dobson gestured for him to sit down, sitting in one of the old worn armchairs himself, He began.

'Scott, I'm sorry to come around unannounced, but I had to see you after you ran out of my shop earlier. I did ring the police,' Scott's face dropped. 'And I spoke to a friend of mine at the station.' Mr Dobson continued 'you see, the watch was stolen from my shop yesterday in a break-in, I'm so glad you got it back for me, I have asked my policeman friend to have a look at it. Now I know it will have your prints on it...'

'No it won't,' butted in Scott, 'I was wearing my gloves so I didn't actually touch it.'

'Well now, that's great thinking Scott,' Mr Dobson looked relieved.

'I...I... didn't do it on purpose, it was cold...' Scott drifted off, feeling like a fool.

'Don't worry Scott, you know you did the right thing by coming to see me, you never know you could have helped catch the burglar.' This cheered Scott up and he managed a slight smile.

At this point Dave backed into the living room, with three steaming mugs of tea.

'Oh thank you Dave that's lovely,' taking the mug Mr Dobson sipped it slowly.

'So what is it you want with my Scott, Mr Dobson?' Dave asked gulping down his own tea. Scott glanced at Mr Dobson with a worried look on his face and slowly shook his head. He understood.

'Oh he's such a good boy; he was just helping me out with the history of a particular item. You see my eyesight's not as good as it use to be, and a young boy like Scott, well he's as sharp as ever.' At this Dave sat up-right in his chair, proud of the compliment given to his son.

Finishing his cup of tea, Mr Dobson set down the cup on the armchair and got up, 'I need to leave now as I have business to attend to, thank you for your hospitality.' Scott and Dave saw him to the door, and watched as he walked down the path.

While Mr Dobson was round Dave's house, Inspector Bradford was organising for fingerprints to be dusted from the watch. He wanted to speak to Scott, but knew if he did he might scare him off, as he had never met him before, plus this Mr Dobson seemed to be doing a good job with him so far. Suddenly the phone rang, it was the desk sergeant saying that a Mr Dobson wanted to see him, 'I was just thinking about him, send him up, thanks.'

'Ah Inspector Bradford, thank you for seeing me,' said Mr Dobson sitting down opposite the desk, feeling slightly intimidated and uncomfortable, probably exactly how they want you to feel, in a police station he thought. 'I spoke with Scott earlier today, so I thought I would let you know the outcome.'

Mr Dobson told inspector Bradford how Scott had found the watch and brought it into his shop. They chatted for about half an hour before Inspector Bradford had to excuse himself for a meeting and Mr Dobson had to get back to work.

The next day Inspector Bradford was handed an envelope containing the results of the fingerprints from the watch. He was a tad surprised at what he saw, but knew exactly where they would find the culprit. Calling in PC's Greene and Gilliam, he explained the situation to them, and asked them to get two squad cars ready as they were to make the arrest today. 'Sir, do you think he could be dangerous? Will we need back-up?' PC Amanda Gilliam asked.

'No Amanda, I don't believe he is, scared and foolish but not dangerous.'

Arriving outside the factory Inspector Bradford instructed PC Greene to take the back factory door; as they expected the culprit to run. They always did. While PC Gilliam and himself went through the main doors to reception.

'Excuse me do you know where we can find Dave Adams?' Inspector Bradford asked.

'Um' the receptionist checked her computer, 'he's in factory one, if you go up that corridor and through the door, turn left, walk down the far wall and he should be there. Can I ask what this is about?'

'I'm afraid not, sorry,' they both turned away and walked down the corridor, knowing that as soon as Dave saw them he would know the games up and run. And what do you know, that's exactly what he did. Panicking Dave headed for the back door, as he shouldered it open he fell straight into PC Greene's arms, struggling to free himself, they got into a bit of a scuffle on the shingle kicking up dust, but Inspector Bradford and PC Gilliam were right behind him. He knew he had no chance, three against one, even if one of them was a woman, so he just slumped to the floor. Cuffing him, Inspector Bradford read Dave his rights. PC's Greene and Gilliam picked him up and escorted him to the waiting police car; his head was bowed in utter shame.

Back at the station Dave was lead into one of the interview rooms, Inspector Bradford explained why he had been arrested, and about the fingerprints found on the watch. Tired and exhausted Dave gave up freely. While he was confessing, Scott was being driven to the police station.

'So... Why do I have to go in?' Scott asked.

'Inspector Bradford will explain everything when we get there, don't worry lad your not in any trouble.' Scott sat in silence staring out the window the rest of the way.

Inspector Bradford was waiting for them when they arrived, 'Hello Scott.'

'Hi Inspector, what's going on?'

'Come on in and I'll tell you.'

Once they were settled in one of the interview rooms, Inspector Bradford told Scott about his Dad's confession.

'No, that's not true! My Dad wouldn't do any of that, he works hard down the factory, he's a good man.' Cried Scott.

'It's ok Scott, I'm sorry you've had to go through this, but your Dad has confessed. I'm afraid it's true.'

'What's going to happen now?' Scott sat with his head in his hands.

'Well, I'm afraid your Dad has been charged.'

'What about me?'

'It'll be ok Scott, try not to worry too much.' Inspector Bradford stood up.

'I want to see him,'

'I think we can arrange that.'

Fifteen minutes later Scott sat opposite his Dad, with two PC's keeping guard behind him.

'Hi Dad,'

'Hi Scott, lad, how are you doing?'

'Ok, what's going on Dad? That copper told me you committed a burglary? Is it true?'

'I'm afraid so son, I know it was a stupid thing to do, and I know I shouldn't make any excuses for it, but I kind of did it for us...'

'What?' Scott cried.

'Well, I didn't want you to miss out on anything; since your Mum left you've been so unhappy,'

'But Dad....'

'No let me finish son, I need to get all this out. I know how unhappy you've been, and you mean the world to me. I'd do anything. I was feeling really quite desperate, and well... I did some really stupid things. I didn't want you to go without at school, all your school friends have the latest fashions and computer games, I wanted you to have them too. I'm so sorry. I didn't mean for it to get this far, I wanted to give you everything you deserve. I wanted you to fit in at school and not be left out. I know it's stupid but, I wasn't really thinking straight, you know I love you son, so very much.'

'I know Dad and I know you always want to get me the latest stuff, but really I don't want all that. I don't really care, you know I would give everything up to have you home Dad, you're more important than all that materialistic stuff.'

'Oh son you don't have to say that...'

'No Dad, I'm serious, I don't care. All I want is you!' Cut in Scott.

Tears started to run down Dave's face and he reached across the table to embrace his son. A few moments later Scott pulled back and asked, 'So Dad, can I ask a question?'

'Sure son,'

'Was that you who dropped the watch up the park?'

'How did you know about that?' Dave sat back in his chair.

'I was there, sorry Dad,'

'Son was that you? My God, sorry, I didn't mean to scare you like that. I tripped on what looked like a torch or something solid anyway, and dropped the watch, and then I heard the rustling in the bush and thought I'd been caught. I just wanted to scare them... Or as I now know it was you.'

'Come on, Scott.' Inspector Bradford laid his hand on Scott's shoulder, 'It's time to go now.'

Scott pulled away from his Dad.

'Everything's going to be alright son, and don't you worry.' Dave smiled, but it didn't quite reach his eyes.

'I know Dad,' Scott smiled back.

Back in the waiting room he sat in silence, running everything through his mind, as Mr Dobson came through the station doors, 'Ah, hello Scott, Inspector Bradford called me and explained everything, how are you holding up?' Mr Dobson sat down next to him.

'Not to well really mister, you know my Dad only robbed your shop for me, he wanted to give me everything I need, so I don't feel left out at school. But you know I think I would be left out anyway, I've never really fitted in, Dad shouldn't have done what he did, but, I know he was only thinking of me.'

'I know Scott, and I've come in today to drop the charges against your father, only the watch he took had any value and I've now got that back haven't I? He didn't break anything, and I think it wouldn't do you any good to have him in prison, now would it.'

'Oh thanks mister that would be amazing!' Scott beamed. Then his smile faded.

'It's my entire fault you know, it was my torch Dad tripped on, it's my fault he's here.'

'Don't say that lad; it would have all come out eventually. You know I believe this whole incident may just well bring you and your father closer together.' Mr Dobson patted Scott's hand in what he hoped was a comforting gesture.

'You really think so?' Scott's heart lifted.

'I do indeed. I'm going to have to have a word with your father though, about what he did, but first of all let me go and sort out the paperwork and see if we can get him out of here.' Leaving Scott on his own Mr Dobson approached the desk sergeant.

Some time later while Scott had started to doze on the reception chairs, Dave was lead through to the front desk, and asked to sign out. As he collected his stuff he looked over his shoulder and gave Scott a small smile as he began to stir. 'Well,' Dave said as he put his arm round Scott's shoulders 'Am I forgiven son?'

'Yeah sure Dad'

'Come on lets go home.'

Mr Dobson watched with a smile as Dave and Scott walked out the door. He saw a close bond had formed between father and son, which could now never be broken.

# Beyond the Grave

'You know, I just love the snow,' Tiffany said smiling up at Andy. Pulling her closer he wrapped his arm around her. 'I know you do honey, it has been a great night tonight hasn't it?'

'Yeah, I really enjoyed it.' Tiffany absentmindedly started to twirl a piece of her long blonde hair around her finger as they walked. 'I still can't believe the twins turned thirteen today, I remember when they were little babies and I babysat them, oh, that makes me sound so old!'

They were making their way back to Tiffany's house, taking the short cut through the churchyard. It was a black night with the moon hiding behind the clouds, peeping out every now and then to cast an eerie glow over the tombstones. Not many people walked through the churchyard this late at night, Tiffany usually opted not to either, as it gave her the creeps, but it did have its perks. It gave her and Andy some along time. It was somewhere to make out, away from her parents' house and their prying eyes.

Lost in her dreamy thoughts, of graves and ghouls, Tiffany didn't realise that Andy had stopped walking; it took her a couple of steps to notice he wasn't by her side. Turning round to look at him standing stock still, she saw that he was as white as a ghost.

'Are you alright? You look a bit pale.' Tiffany probed. He didn't move or answer, he just pointed at the ground a few yards away. As Tiffany followed his line of vision she caught her breath. On the ground lay an elderly lady, who didn't look as though she was breathing. Andy whispered 'Can you see what I see? She looks dead.'

'Uh uh.' was all Tiffany could reply, her eyes wide with fear.

Andy moved slowly towards the lady on the ground, not wanting to make a sound, but not quite sure why. He gradually bent down and reached out wanting to feel a pulse, when a shadow flitted beyond the graves and made his heart momentarily jump into his throat.

'Tiffany!' Jumping at her own name now, how stupid she felt.

'What?' she replied.

Andy backed away from the old lady and moved towards Tiffany 'I saw a shadow over the back; I'm going to check it out. If anyone's there, then they may know something about this old lady. Check to see if she's still breathing and call an ambulance will you?'

Tiffany shrugged, 'Sure. She looks dead anyway, I don't know what good an ambulance is going to do.' Pulling her coat tightly around her, she really didn't want to touch the old lady.

'Just do it, will you?' Andy sighed and walked into the darkness.

'Fine, I'll do it,' Tiffany huffed.

As Andy walked off, Tiffany got out her mobile, 'Damn no signal, now what!' Convinced the old lady was dead, Tiffany looked around. Suddenly aware at how isolated and cold it was getting. She could see her hot breath turning into mist.

She was also getting jumpy, movements in the bushes and trees that she wasn't sure were really there, were making her feel slightly paranoid, or maybe her mind was just playing tricks on her. But what ever it was, she didn't see or hear the old lady slowly getting up behind her.

'Hello dear, what are you doing out here?'

'Ahhhhh,' Tiffany screamed, eyes wide, her breath caught in her throat and she hit the floor with a thud; knocking herself out cold with shock.

'Oh dear.' looking down at Tiffany with concern the old lady was reaching out to feel for a pulse and make sure she was ok when Andy came running back.

'Hey what's going on? What have you done?' he hit the floor on his knees next to Tiffany and checked her pulse.

'I don't really know, I said hello and she fainted, is she going to be ok?' asked the old lady, concerned.

'Tiffany, Tiffany can you hear me?' Andy called out. She didn't move, but he could feel a strong pulse and knew she would be ok, having known her to faint before. He turned to the old lady.

'What the hell happened? We thought you were dead!'

'Dead? Me no,' the old lady faltered, 'I, I'm not dead, I think I must have just fallen asleep, I came to visit my husband's grave.'

'But it's snowing and your not wearing a coat, you look like you're dressed for summer, who are you?' Andy frowned.

'My name is Flora Littlekit.'

Tiffany suddenly began to stir and Andy's attention was diverted.

'Are you ok honey? How do you feel?' he asked.

'I'm, I'm ok I think,' she Mumbled 'What happened?' Tiffany held her head as she sat up, remembering the dead lady who spoke to her, slowly she looked up at a set of piercing blue eyes in an old face staring down at her. 'Who are you are, are you dead? Am I dead? I feel confused!'

'No dear, as I was explaining to your young man, I'm not dead, I must have fallen asleep, I'm just visiting my husband's grave, as I do all the time.'

'Ok fine, but you didn't explain why you're in a t-shirt and shorts when it's snowing?' Andy quizzed her, staring hard.

'Is it? Oh dear me.' Flora looked around her feeling confused. Andy shook his head as he bent down to help Tiffany up. 'Great, we've got a nut job on our hands here,' he whispered.

'Don't say that! She's just a bit confused and lonely is all.' Tiffany pushed herself up and walked towards Flora, 'Do you need any help getting home? It really is getting quite cold now, and as you don't have a coat you must be freezing.'

Looking down at herself the old lady said, 'you know I don't feel cold, quite the opposite really, it feels like a summers day.' Tiffany and Andy exchanged knowing looks.

'Let's get you home, where do you live?' Tiffany probed.

'By the duck pond, my Harry and I use to love feeding the ducks; I still do it on my own, now my Harry's gone, they're such funny creatures at times, those ducks.'

Andy looked at her confused, 'Are you sure? The duck pond was filled in three years ago.'

An Exasperated Flora looked Andy square in the eyes, 'No, no, no, it can't have been. I was there this morning. You know, I think I'll be just fine getting home, Thank you.'

'Ok. Are you sure you will be ok?' Tiffany asked concerned.

'Yes dear I'll be fine,' she shuffled past them and through the gravestones. Tiffany and Andy watched her go, completely speechless. They could hear her mumbling to herself as she went, 'Filled In the duck pond! Never. They would never do that. Filled in the duck pond he says!'

'Wow, she was a strange lady, you know, I think you're right, a little crazy too.' Tiffany said shaking her head as they headed in the other direction.

Andy nodded, 'Yeah she sure was. I still can't believe she was wearing a t-shirt in this weather!'

'I know, madness.'

'Yeah.' Andy wrapped his arm around Tiffany's shoulders, and said 'She's gone now anyway, let's go home and warm up it's damn freezing out here.'

The next morning Tiffany trundled down stairs in her dressing gown to grab a cup of coffee, and try to shake her hangover, but she had a feeling that her headache was really down to not sleeping at all that night, as she couldn't get Flora of her mind.

Tiffany's Dad was sitting at the kitchen table reading the morning newspaper, when she walked in. 'Hi Dad, how's it going?'

'Morning honey, did you have a good night last night?' he folded his newspaper and picked up his coffee.

'Yeah it was good,' Tiffany screwed up her face.

'What's up love you look like you have something on your mind?'

'Yeah well, we stumbled onto this strange lady last night when we took the short cut through the church yard.'

'Ok. Who was she? What was strange about her?' his interest peaked.

'She said her name was Flora Littlekit, does that mean anything to you?'

'Well it does ring a bell, I can't think why though,' he searched his mind for how he knew that name. 'I don't know. Anyway, what was so strange about her?' he asked again.

'Well for a starters we thought she was dead, we found her lying on the ground hardly moving.' Tiffany then told her Dad everything that had happened the previous night. As he was a policeman she knew he would be interested, he always loved a bit of a mystery.

Tiffany finished with, 'She just walked away from us, mumbling, I think Andy upset her, when he said the duck pond had been filled in. it was strange as she seemed to fade, but I guess that could have been an illusion as it was dark and the snow was getting heavier.'

'Well honey, you're right, that does sound strange, and she definitely said she lived near, and fed the ducks? Because Andy was right the duck pond was filled in three years ago. I've got to say though, Flora's name sounds familiar, I'm sure I know it from somewhere, maybe one of my old cases. Let me have a think, I'll just have a shower and get dressed, then I'll get back to you.' he scraped back the chair and left the kitchen, she could hear his slippers clomping up the wooden stairs.

Tiffany was at the table eating a bowl of cereal when Andy walked in, 'Hi honey, are you ok?' He asked.

'Yeah, I'm fine Andy, thanks, I spoke to Dad about Flora this morning, and he thinks he knows her from somewhere, he's going to have a think and check it out for me.'

'You know, I don't want you to get to hooked up on her, she was just a crazy old lady, I bet she's from an old peoples home, just escaped.'

'I know I know,' Tiffany sighed, lets just wait and see what Dad says about it.'

'Fine.' Andy helped himself to some breakfast, and they both ate in silence while he read Tiffany's Dad's leftover newspaper. When Tiffany's Dad came back in he helped himself to some more coffee. 'Hey Mr. Jenkins how are you?'

'Morning Andy, I'm doing well thanks.'

'Hey Dad, Have you thought any more about Flora Littlekit?' Tiffany asked eagerly.

'I have and I even rang a colleague of mine whose been on the force a lot of years, he also recognised the name and dug out an old file for me while I was in the shower, I don't think you're going to quite believe this, but your Flora Littlekit died in August 1979!'

'What! Dad no, that can't be true, don't be silly, we spoke to her last night!'

'Yeah seriously Mr. Jenkins, we really did see her,' Andy had to sit back down again, feeling a bit light headed. He had got up to get more toast.

Mr. Jenkins continued, 'I know honey but listen, let me explain. Flora Littlekit really did die in August 1979.

She was unfortunately attacked in the graveyard you found her in. From police records, it looks like it was a mugging that went wrong. She tried to fight off her attacker, but he pushed her so hard she fell and hit her head on a tombstone. She died there and then from her injuries.'

'That's so strange, so what you're saying is that we spoke to a ghost? Is that right Dad?'

'I'm afraid so love, there have been several reported sightings of an old lady lying in the grave yard, over the years, she died before she got to her husband Harry's grave.'

'Wow, that's pretty amazing, it's like she has unfinished business, because she never made it, she keeps coming back trying to get there, wow that's surreal,' Tiffany got up and put her empty plate in the sink.

Andy had been sitting quietly, but decided to say something as he knew Tiffany well, and could imagine what she was thinking. 'There's nothing you can do about it though Tiff. Some spirits are still here because of unfinished business before they died. They can't cross over properly.' Mr. Jenkins raised his eyebrow at Andy. 'My Mum's into all the spiritual stuff, she's addicted to all the ghostly day-time TV shows.' He said in way of an explanation.

'So what can we do?' Tiffany needed to do something, she felt so sorry for Flora.

'Well,' Tiffany's Dad said, 'The sightings have had no pattern to them, so we don't know when she will appear again.'

'I think the only thing that I can do, is maybe visit her husbands grave and lay flowers, I know I didn't have anything to do with Flora's death, I mean I wasn't even born! But I need to do something; maybe if she sees that someone else cares, it might just give her the peace she needs to cross over.' Tiffany said thoughtfully.

'You know I think that's a great idea Tiff,' Andy got up and gave her a big hug.

'Thanks Dad. For looking into this for me, I mean.' She turned back to Andy, 'Do you want to go down the florist and help me pick out some nice flowers?'

'Sure, get dressed and we'll head on out,' Andy said gently.

'Excellent.' Tiffany smiled at him.

'Right I'm off out now, going to meet some old force friends for a coffee, and then maybe a nice lunchtime pint, I'll see you two later. Will you both be here for tea?'

'Yeah, sure will be Dad.'

An hour later they were entering the churchyard with a lovely bouquet of white lilies to lay onto Harry Littlekit's grave. Tiffany felt a shiver run down her spine as she placed them next to his gravestone. She could literally feel the calm in the air, peaceful and quiet. She felt that Flora was watching them, could feel her eyes following them. Smiling to herself she felt a huge sense of satisfaction, that she was helping someone from the other side to pass over and finally rest in peace.

# Emily Black

Emily Black is your typical teenager. She loves high street fashion, make up, listening to her favourite CD's, hanging out with her mates and of course boys.

She lives with her Mum. Who she doesn't always get on with, and secretly loves to bits but of course would never tell her that. They live together in a recently renovated Victorian terrace house.

This particular day felt a bit different when Emily woke, it was a Sunday and the sun was streaming through the small gap in her pale pink curtains highlighting the strip of dancing dust, lying back on her pillow Emily wanted to be happy, no school after all, but something wasn't quite right.

Emily's Nan had always told her they had psychics in the family, she just thought it was an old wives tale; she believed her Nan told her so she could appear to look cool, Emily loved it really, but being a teenager meant the rules were against it.

The smell of her Mum baking eventually got her out of bed, and all the bad thoughts vanished from her mind, dragging her extra soft turquoise dressing gown on, Emily shuffled down stairs into the kitchen, the sweet smell made her mouth water, as she got her self a glass of juice.

'So, Mum, what are you making?' dropping into one of the dining chairs, she tried to stick her finger in the mixing bowl, but got a swift rap on the knuckles with the spatula.

'Hey you! I've made your Nan some rock cakes and two apple pies, you know what she's like when Granddad's away, and she isn't getting any younger.'

'Sure.' Emily put her comfy hood up and laid her head on the table.

'Oh Emily come on, go and have a shower, you can take this lot over there. And...spend a bit of time with your Nan.'

'Oh Mum, really? Do I have to? I want to go out with my mate's today,' moaned Emily.

'Yes you do, now go do as you're told. It's school holidays so you have plenty of other days to lay about doing nothing with your friends.'

'fine!' Emily stomped up stairs and took a rather longer than usual shower.

'Right, I'm ready,' Emily huffed back into the kitchen.

'Good girl, you'll be ok, you know your Nan loves it when you visit. She tells the whole family what a wonderful granddaughter she has, just because you go round there.'

'Well, ok, I guess I don't mind it too much.' Emily's gaze dropped to the floor, while her Mum smiled to her self.

'Here you go, put these in your backpack, and you're ready to go, oh hang on, I need you to pop to the grocery store on your way, your Nan called yesterday afternoon, she needs a few things, here's a list, and some money.'

'Ok.' Emily slid her bag of the table, and grabbed the bits her Mum handed out.

Setting of out the front door, she slammed it behind her; just hearing the muffled voice of her Mum through it, shouting to be careful 'and stick to the main roads!' Emily started to feel guilty for being so grumpy with her, she didn't mean it, and she hated to think she had upset her Mum, but she just couldn't help it, hopefully a walk to the shops would cheer her up.

Emily wanted to get to her Nan's and back again as soon as possible, as she should be going to the cinema with friends to see the new Harry Potter, but she hadn't told her Mum yet, and wasn't sure she would allow her to go.

Emily's Nan and Granddad lived in a new block of houses, all with lovingly pruned tiny square front gardens. They were built specifically for people over 65. She did love her grandparents very much, and was thankful that their new home was closer; the walk to the old house was a nightmare. But this new house smelt a little bit too clean, it was more like a hospital, disinfectant smell, magnolia walls, beige carpets, and ramps to the front door. It even had handles in the hall way and bathroom. The whole row looked identical; it had no personality about it. Maybe that's just because they are new, once people start to re-decorate and do the gardens they'll look a lot nicer, thought Emily.

Even though she knew they were both ancient, Emily didn't believe they should be in an old people's home just yet.

Lost in her thoughts walking down the street, she didn't notice the man staring at her from the other side of the road, until he had crossed it and was standing in front of her.

'Good Morning Emily.'

'Oh! Good Morning!' startled, Emily stared at the man not wanting to forget her manners; her Mum would be furious if she did "Manners don't cost a thing" she was always saying.

He looked vaguely familiar, but she had no idea how she knew him. As if reading her mind he smiled and said 'You don't remember me, do you?'

'Sorry, I don't.'

'Never mind, that's ok, it has been a long time, my name is Seth, I'm good friends with your Nan Sylvia.'

'Really, I'm now on my way to see my Nan, I have cakes! She's feeling a bit lonely because Granddad is away this week,' Emily blurted out.

'Ah, I see. So you've been busy baking?'

'No, my Mum made the cakes. I'm sorry but I better get going, I need to stop in town first.'

'That's fine Emily, maybe we'll meet again.' Interesting he thought; Very interesting. She'll be in town a while, a young girl like her can't resist the temptation of shopping, he thought.

He was a bit strange, thought Emily, as she walked away from Seth. But she soon shook all thoughts of him from her mind.

While Emily detoured to the local shop, Seth headed straight to Sylvia's house. He had planned to go there anyway, as he knew she was a very old fragile lady just ripe for the picking, but knowing she was on her own made it all the more easier.

Seth hurried, picking up his pace; he rounded the last corner and saw Emily's Nan's home.

'Knock, Knock!'

A few seconds past and then, 'Who is it?' called Sylvia, as she unbolted the door.

'Hi Sylvia, It's Seth, Seth Carpenter. I'm Rita Haughton's son?'

'Oh, I remember, hang on,' she called back. 'This lock is a bit stiff, there it goes.' The door swung wide open.

'I thought I'd pop over. See how you're doing these days, Mum sends her regards.' Seth stepped inside glancing round the large living room.

'That's lovely, come in come in, I'll put the kettle on, and how is your Mum these days?' Sylvia headed towards the kitchen.

'She's doing well thank you. I know it has been a while now, but I was in the area.' Seth stood in the door-way with his hands behind his back taking in everything in the living room, trying to price it up on the black market. Well, what he would get for it down the local pub, anyway.

'My young Granddaughter's coming to visit at some point today,' Sylvia continued, as she wandered back into the living room with a tea towel drying a china cup, 'she's a lovely girl, I believe you've met her before?'

'Oh yes, I remember, it was some years ago though,' Seth replied.

'Yes, she's quite the young lady now, nearly thirteen; they grow up so quickly, anyway how about that tea.'

'That sounds great,' Seth smiled.

As she busied herself back in the kitchen with the kettle, her back was turned, Seth silently picked up a ghastly cat ornament that sat on the bureau, guessing it was probably worthless, he crept up behind her, raised both hands high in the air, and brought the ornament down in one swift hard movement onto the back of her head, knocking her out cold. The china cup she held shattered on the flagstone kitchen floor.

Trying to compose himself, heart beating, he hoisted Sylvia up under her arms and dragged her across the kitchen, through the living room, to the cupboard under the stairs. After a few minutes struggling with her limp body, he managed to stuff her inside it.

'Excellent!' he proclaimed to the empty room, rubbing his hands together.

As soon as Seth started to unplug the DVD player, his pockets stuffed with silverware, he heard the garden gate creaking. Peering through the curtains he saw Emily walking down the path, and his heart started pounding.

'Oh God, Oh God, I thought I'd have ages!'

A thousand thoughts raced through his head, what am I going to do? She can't know I'm here; I can't let her see what I've done. She can't ring the police; I'm not going back there! Panicking, he opened the cupboard that he had rammed Emily's Nan into just a few moments ago, and noticed she was still breathing. He breathed a small sigh of relief to himself. He was no killer, but he did get a thrill from what he was doing, the adrenaline rush was just amazing, and no matter how many times he told himself this was going to be the last time, there was always one more.

'Well if it's good enough for granny, it's good enough for Emily.' Pushing the door too, he picked up a weighty figurine just as Emily knocked on the door. Standing with his back to the wall, arms raised, he waited for the door to open.

'Nan? Are you ok? The doors unlocked!' Emily moved the door open slowly, peering in, as Seth adjusted his position, unfortunately he made the floor boards creak, ever so slightly, but Emily heard it, she gasped as she looked up, just as Seth brought down the figurine. Emily jerked her head sharply backwards and he missed, stumbling forward he dropped the figurine; with a thud it hit the floor. He grabbed Emily by the shoulders, and pulled her into the living room. As she struggled to get free, she managed to get in a swift kick to his shins which momentarily stunned him, but he had a solid grip, and didn't let go. Pushing her against the wall Emily banged her head. Seth desperately wanted to get her to stop struggling; Emily flung her arms in every direction, trying to get him to loosen his grip, she was finally proving to be too much for him. He pushed her again with all his strength; she hit her head on the door frame, knocking herself unconscious. She slid down the wall into a heap on the floor.

Breathing deeply and wiping the sweat from his brow he picked Emily up in his arms, and laid her down next to her Nan in the cupboard, making sure to lock it.

'Right lets get on with this,' he said to himself, and set to work again grabbing as much electrical gear that he could carry, plus any jewellery or ornaments that looked valuable. Not that Seth knew much about expensive ornaments, so he just grabbed the ugliest ones, figuring they must be valuable.

Meanwhile Sylvia's neighbour, Quincy Smythe; who happened to be a very nosey, regimented, retired navel officer; saw a man he didn't recognise going into her house, and witnessed the scuffle with Sylvia's granddaughter.

Quincy was known for jumping the gun, and calling the police for the smallest of matters. Fortunately for his Neighbour, this time he was correct. He decided to take no risks, and called a local policeman that he mistakenly considered to be a friend.

About five minutes later PC Stinson pulled up outside Sylvia's home, in his new unmarked police car, he couldn't see anything untoward, and to be honest didn't expect to, but they were obliged to investigate any alleged crimes.

PC Stinson cursed Quincy Smythe under his breath, annoyed that his lunch had been rudely interrupted by the local busy body. He knew that he shouldn't be nasty about the old guy, after all he had fought for this country and been awarded some pretty impressive medals, but he just couldn't help thinking that his life would be a little more easier without Quincy on the phone every five god damn minutes, with his latest conspiracy theory.

Deciding to quickly check it out for Quincy's sake, and hopefully keep him happy for a little while, plus for his own sanity, PC Stinson got out of his car, careful to lock it behind him and walked up the path to Sylvia's front door. His mind was on his pasta bake going cold back at the station, when he noticed the front door wasn't shut properly, he eased it open ever so slightly. As silently as possible, he peered in through the crack and spotted a man dressed in dark clothes. He scanned his brain for a name but realised he had no idea who this guy was.

Having been the neighbourhood bobby for the past Twelve years he knew pretty much everyone on the street, but this guy he didn't know, and that made him suspicious. He slowly drew his gun, held it to chest height, and pushed the door open wide enough to get his gun through.

Seth picked up an expensive looking vase, and held it up to the light.

Easing the front door open a bit more, PC Stinson scanned the living room for any accomplices.

Seth began rummaging through the sideboard drawers, he had his back turned to PC Stinson, and was concentrating on ignoring the banging coming from the under stairs cupboard.

Suddenly. PC Stinson threw open the door.

'Freeze!'

Seth spun round in such shock; he dropped everything in his hands, the tiny china Elephant salt and pepper shakers, shattered on the floor. Neither man moved.

'Hands up now!' shouted PC Stinson. He looked around him because he could hear banging coming from somewhere.

A series of muffled bangs rang out! 'Bang, rattle Bang!'

'What the hells that? Hey I said don't move!' Seth froze mid step toward the door.

'Turn around slowly,' Seth did as he was told. The officer advanced forward, grabbed his wrist roughly, and handcuffed him. He then grabbed his radio from his belt and called in the burglary, to the station.

The banging began to get a bit louder 'Bang, Bang!'

After pulling Seth to the stairs and passing the cuffs through the banisters to secure him, PC Stinson went to investigate the banging in the cupboard under the stairs, only to discover Emily and her Nan standing in the dark, fists raised about to bang on the door again.

'Oh my God, thank God you're here, I thought we would never get out of there!' Nan exclaimed loudly, trying to catch her breath.

'Thanks Mister,' said Emily quietly.

'No problem little lady, are either of you hurt?'

'No, we are both fine thank you,' replied Sylvia, 'a little shaken up but not hurt.'

'That's good, I have to get this guy down to the station now, are you both going to be ok for a while? I've called in the burglary; someone should be here shortly to take statements down from both of you.'

Both Emily and her Nan looked at Seth. He looked so pathetic, sad and defeated, handcuffed to the banisters, they almost felt sorry for him, but that didn't last long.

PC Stinson collected Seth from the banister, bade good day to Emily and her Nan and left pulling Seth behind him, but not before leaving his card.

Both Sylvia and Emily stood at the door watching as PC Stinson and Seth drove away, sirens blaring. After shutting the door, Sylvia said, 'Well, I'm glad that's all over, are you ok dear? I was really worried about you in there,' she gestured towards the cupboard.

'Just a little claustrophobic really, and a headache but nothing major. It was scary though, I could hear him out here and didn't know what he was going to do with us.'

'I know dear, awful situation to be in. Oh dear lord! What are we going to tell your mother?'

'I don't know Nan, do we have to? She will only worry.'

'We do I'm afraid, but it'll be ok, we can tell her over tea this afternoon. By the way do you fancy a cup of tea?'

All thoughts of the movie she should have been watching later on with her friends had completely fallen out of her mind.

'Thanks Nan that would be great,' she smiled.

Knowing that things could have gone really wrong today, Emily wanted to spend as much time with her beloved Grandma as possible.

# Miranda Frost

Miranda knew she would have to knock at some point, knowing it was inevitable if she wanted to lead a normal life, but now didn't feel like the right time. She stood at the gate staring at the bungalow, searing the image into her mind. Her heart beating so fast it felt like it was going to explode. Shaking her head out of her day dream, Miranda decided today wasn't the day, maybe tomorrow? Turning around she walk away, kicking her self inside for chickening out when she was so close.

Pulling her jacket collar up against the bitter wind that seemed to have crept up on her, Miranda strode back towards town.

She found her-self walking past the rows of shops that felt so familiar, yet she felt alienated from everything, as though she was invisible and everyone was just getting on with their lives, and completely ignoring her.

She hated this town, and everyone in it. That was the real reason she left all those years ago, the people here were a bunch of losers, all the young ones cared about was getting their next fix and the opening time of the local pub. The old people only moved here to die, so many old people, and all the new, old people retirement flats that were being built, were filling up quickly. No new houses for young families. But no one expected any respectable young people to come here, ever.

No one seemed to have any ambition and if you did you were laughed at and told you were living with your head in the clouds, being here made Miranda feel depressed.

Spotting her car she quickened her pace, jumping in, she locked her doors, and turned on her CD player. Breathing a small sigh, it made her feel better being in her car, in safer territory.

Gripping the steering wheel she left her depressing home town, and headed towards the bypass. Finally she started to feel her spirits lift, and her heart steady out. Miranda was singing along to some of her favourite tracks by the time she got home.

The sun was out and life seemed good again.

Two weeks later Miranda found herself sitting on her sofa in her silent living room, staring into space, she had been feeling sick and depressed even more than usual, and knew she was stressed, depressed and extremely unhappy.

Reaching absentmindedly for her anti-depressants, her sleeve caught a glass of water, knocking it over, she jumped up in shock, knocking the table as the water soaked her jeans and the pills went flying all over the room.

Standing in the middle of the silent room, with soaked jeans and pills woven into her carpet, Miranda could feel her face tightening and her eyes sting, as the first tear fell, falling to her knees she couldn't stop herself crying. It needed to be let out. She curled up into a ball on the living room floor and just cried, huge great big gulping sobs of tears for what felt like hours, she couldn't stop. Eventually she moved to the sofa, pulled up an old crocheted blanket, and cried herself to sleep.

Waking the next morning with a horrible stiff neck, Miranda dragged herself into the shower, standing there with the steaming hot water hitting her face, her eye caught the razor on the sink, and suddenly she was thinking how easy it would be to just end it all right here and now.

She reached for it, but then changed her mind, not wanting to go there again. She had been this low before, when she lived with her parents; no one ever listened to her, not her Mum or Dad, friends, family even boyfriends. She was expected to just go along with whatever anyone else wanted to do and like it. She wasn't allowed her own voice, she felt claustrophobic living like that, trapped in her own mind, not daring to speak out, that's why she ran away.

But now she had responsibilities, she couldn't just think about herself anymore, she knew she needed to go back, if just for a day, to show her family she had changed and hoping they had too.

Her parents weren't too bad, they just conformed to the masses, she couldn't hate them for that, so many people do it now, the only life they know how to live, the life of a sheep.

Dressing in her favourite jeans and jumper, she wanted to look good but didn't quite have the confidence to dress in anything nice or fashionable, so she went for her trusted favourites.

Miranda popped next door to Mr's Murphy's.

'Morning Honey, how are you feeling today?' Mr's Murphy asked.

'Not to bad thanks, I'm going to try again today, but this time I want to take Jamie with me.'

'Really, are you sure that's wise?' Miranda raised her eyebrows, as Mr's Murphy raised her hands in a peaceful gesture, 'you know I'm only looking out for you.'

Smiling, Miranda said, 'I know, thank you. You've been my rock these last few years, Thank you for looking after Jamie so much, I don't know what I would have done without you, but I'm going to do it this time. I need to see them, its felt like something has been missing for such a long time, I keep pushing it to the back of my mind, because my heads saying hate them but my heart says you can't do that their your parents, so I'm going to follow my heart. It may get broken again but I've got to try.'

Mr's Murphy eyed her with concern and uncertainty, 'Ok, but you know where I am if you need me though, don't you? I'll go and get him.'

Standing In the kitchen on her own, Miranda looked around her. Sudden doubts flooding her mind, 'no' she wouldn't let them cloud her judgement pushing them out she stood firm and waited for Jamie.

A few minutes later she saw that gorgeous familiar smile walk through the door.

'Mummy, look what I made.' Jamie held up an empty toilet roll with some coloured paper stuck to it, 'wow that's wonderful baby, have you had a good time round Aunty Murphy's?'

'Yep,' he replied, staring proudly at his toilet roll.

Miranda looked up at Mr's Murphy and mouthed the word thank you. 'Right you, were going on a trip today, to see some people... say bye, baby,'

'Bye bye Aunty Murphy.'

Mr's Murphy hugged him tight, and smiled at Miranda as they both left.

The journey to town was largely a silent one, thankfully thought Miranda. Mr's Murphy had worn Jamie out which meant he was asleep most of the way.

Miranda's thoughts soon drifted back to her parents. Knowing that today was going to be the first time she has seen them since running away five years previous, wondering if they had aged much. Hopefully not, her Mum, Carolyn, had always been very glamorous and popular. Her Dad, George, was hardly ever home, always away on business: Japan, America, Germany, and China, all over the world, which meant she was unable to really form a close bond with him.

Unfortunately history does tend to repeat itself. Jamie will hardly see his father either, but that was more to do with him being a womanising idiot, who slept with the wrong mans wife once to often, and ended up getting himself thrown in prison for six years, but that's a whole other story.

Miranda decided to keep her heart closed, she was doing this for Jamie, and he had the right to see where his Mum came from. To meet his grandparents, it would hopefully answer all the questions she had dreaded for so long, that he had started to ask recently.

Parking a few houses down the street, Miranda breathed deeply, and caught sight of the street sign, on the corner grass verge, hanging on its wooden posts. Someone had sprayed graffiti in florescent pink over the 'Hell' part of the word Hellson Avenue. Hellson, this place really was Hell, thought Miranda, Hell on Earth.

Snapping out of her day dream, she woke up a sleepy Jamie. Lifting him out of the car she carried him down the street to her old home, they slowed to a stop at the gate. Miranda laid her hand on the latch, her heart beating fast. She slowly pushed the old creaky gate open, and walked down the path, a thousand thoughts rushing through her mind.

Gripping Jamie's hand tightly Miranda knocked on the door, wanting to run but felt glued to the spot, the door opened.

'Hi Mum.'

Carolyn froze, one hand still on the door, the other clutching the wall. She still looked glamorous, but now she also looked old and drawn, age had found her. She was wearing a tight pale pink t-shirt over skinny, worn jeans and tottering on her pink fluffy stiletto style house shoes, her hair was bleached blonde and you could see at least two inches of dark roots.

Miranda's first thought, well it was a feeling really, was how familiar and comfortable her Mums presence seemed; even though she looked like she'd seen a ghost.

Carolyn suddenly snapped out of her shocked state, she looked down at little Jamie and her lip started to quiver; Miranda wanted to reach out to her but couldn't bring her self to do it, not just yet.

Carolyn ushered them both inside, leaning and peering from side to side out the front door just before closing it.

'Well, oh my, I'm speechless.' Carolyn's whole body started to shake and tears streamed down her face. She reached shakily into her pocket and pulled out a crumpled packet of Marlboro lights, lighting one she exhaled deeply.

'I see your still smoking!' Miranda said crassly.

'They're lights, and don't lecture me! Do you not realise how worried your father and I have been all these years, we thought you were dead! No letters, no phone call, nothing. We even had the police dredge the lake! For Christ sake...' she hissed.

'Fine, if you're going to be like that...' Miranda headed back toward the door, but Carolyn grabbed her arm before she made it. 'I'm sorry love. You just don't realise what you've put us both through, I'm just glad you're alive.'

'Thanks Mum, I know I probably deserve it but please, not now.' Miranda dared to lay a hand on top of her mothers, her breath held.

'I'll make us a cuppa tea, then you can tell me all about this little soldier here, and where you've been for the last five years.' Carolyn ruffled Jamie's hair and he shied away behind his Mum. Solve the world's problems with a pot of tea, if she could, thought Miranda.

'Have a seat in the living room love, I wont be long...do you still take sugar?'

'No not anymore, thanks.' Miranda looked up at the old wall clock and called out 'The place is looking good Mum, it doesn't appear you've changed it much, obviously the walls are a different colour and you've gone for a more modern look but still it feels the same.'

Miranda suddenly heard a crash from the kitchen, not knowing if she should help, she called out, 'Are you OK in there, do you need me to do anything?'

Carolyn appeared at the doorway 'No, love that's fine I've got it, just a broken handle is all.' She laid the tray of tea and biscuits on a TV dinner tray. Helped her self to the I heart Monday's mug and sat down in a pastel pink crushed velvet armchair.

Miranda sat cautiously opposite her in the matching chair, while little Jamie squeezed himself between his Mum and the chairs arm.

The silence felt solid and static between them, so Miranda decided to break it, 'Where's Dad today?' she asked.

'He's working, meetings in Stuttgart. He's really going to flip when I tell him about your visit today.'

'Is he ok?'

'He's fine, busy with work and all that...Ok, look, I really want to shout at you, because I'm so angry you just ran away like that, where have you been? What have you been living on? Have you been looking after yourself? Where are you living now?'

'Wow, Mum, one at a time please.'

'Fine.' Carolyn straightened in her chair, 'You know you're classed as a missing person; I'm going to have to call the police, tell them you're alive and well.'

'I know Mum, I don't want to cause any more hurt, that's why I've come back, and for little Jamie here, I thought he should know his grandparents.'

'Why have you taken so long to come back? We didn't even know Jamie existed!'

'I know Mum I'm so sorry, I had a lot of issues back then, I'm in a really stable place at the moment, I have a good job and a two bed flat, it's going well.'

'Where did you go when you ran away?'

'I went to London, I had some friends there who put me up for a while, while I got myself together, and it just kind of went on from there. I've been ok, you know, nothing bad has happened to me, I just couldn't be here anymore.'

'Why what did we do so wrong?' Carolyn looked hurt.

'Seriously Mum, you should know! You never cared about me, or that's how it felt at the time. All you cared about was your reputation in this crappy little town.' Miranda gripped the side of the chair.

'Don't say that! It's not true. We cared very much about you.'

'Honestly, you didn't show it.'

'Really Miranda, I can't believe...'

Miranda cut in, 'Mum listen, I was just trying to be honest about how I felt back then, but it was a long time ago now, can we talk about it later when everyone has calmed down a bit?'

'Ok, well I guess you're right. You're here now that's all that matters. We can work through other stuff later, where are you living?'

'Were living about a thirty five minute drive from here, we have a nice place don't we Jamie?' The little boy nodded shyly.

'So Not too far, then.'

'No Mum, not too far.'

'Are we going to see you again?'

'I hope so. Only if you want to see us again, that is?'

'Of course we do, honey, we want to see this little chap as well.' Carolyn smiled at Jamie.

'I want you to get to know him Mum; I want him to know his grandparents.'

They made small talk for another half hour or so. Miranda had decided many days ago that she would only stay an hour, hour and a half max, so when the conversation fell into an uneasy silence she took her chance and broke it.

'We really should be going now.'

'Really, do you have to?'

'I want to take this one step at a time. I'll give you my mobile number so we can arrange another time, how does that sound?' They made their way through to the front door.

'That sounds great honey.' Carolyn picked up the pastel phone block and Miranda jotted down her number and address.

'Oh Mum, please don't cry.' Tears began to stream down Carolyn's face.

'I can't help it. My daughter has come home!' she wailed.

'I know Mum; I'm not going to disappear again this time. Don't worry, I'm not far away.'

'I do love you, you know.'

Miranda was taken aback, 'I don't think I've ever heard you say that before.'

'There's nothing like a daughter running away to make you re-evaluate your life.'

'Oh Mum,' Miranda hugged her Mum tightly on the door step, 'we will be back, I promise.'

Carolyn bent down to hug Jamie, but he shied away, still uncertain of the lady with the big hair, 'It's ok honey, this is your Nan.'

'It is ok, I'm your Nan,' mimicked Carolyn, not quite able to believe that this beautiful blond haired, blue eyed boy was her grandchild.

'Nan,' he said, and looking up to his Mum for approval he stepped forward letting Carolyn embrace him.

Walking back to the car after Carolyn had shut the door, Miranda couldn't help smiling, feeling that a huge weight, and a hefty burden had been lifted from her shoulders. All the way home little Jamie excitedly asked his Mum questions about his new grand parents, which Miranda felt finally happy to try and answer.

Printed in the United Kingdom by
Lightning Source UK Ltd., Milton Keynes
142269UK00001B/58/P